Tom and Pippo See the Moon

PIPPO

HELEN OXENBURY

ALADDIN BOOKS
Macmillan Publishing Company • New York

One night, when it was dark,
I saw the moon shining in the sky.

I asked Daddy all about the moon.
Daddy told me that a man had been
on the moon and he had to get there
in a rocket.
I asked Daddy if
there was anybody
on the moon now,
and Daddy said no.

I think Pippo and I
will go to the moon one day.
We will go in a rocket.

I asked Daddy
if Pippo and I
could go to
the moon, and Daddy said maybe,
but the moon is very far away.

If Pippo and I go to the moon one day, I think Daddy should come, too.

Anyway, tonight I think we will just go to sleep. Maybe we will go to the moon tomorrow.